THE ECONOMIC IMPACT OF
COVID-19

BY EMILY HUDD

CONTENT CONSULTANT
Louphou Coulibaly, PhD
Assistant Professor, Department of Economics
University of Pittsburgh

Core Library

An Imprint of Abdo Publishing
abdobooks.com

Cover image: Times Square in New York City was deserted during
the COVID-19 pandemic.

abdobooks.com

Printed in the United States of America, North Mankato, Minnesota
072020
092020

THIS BOOK CONTAINS
RECYCLED MATERIALS

Cover Photo: Tatiana Stolyarova/Sputnik/AP Images,
Interior Photos: Shutterstock Images, 4–5; iStockphoto, 8, 15, 36, 43; David J. Phillip/AP Images, 10, 45; Rich Pedroncelli/AP/Bloomberg/Getty Images, 12–13; Wilfredo Lee/AP Images, 17; Red Line Editorial, 19, 23; Al Drago/AP Images, 20–21; Aly Song/Reuters/Newscom, 26–27; Fabio Mazzarella/ Sintesi/SIPA/Newscom, 29; Angel Garcia/Bloomberg/Getty Images, 32; Niall Carson/PA Wire URN:53634379/Press Association/AP Images, 34–35; Michele Ursi/Shutterstock Images, 39

Editor: Angela Lim
Series Designer: Jake Nordby

Library of Congress Control Number: 2020936520

Publisher's Cataloging-in-Publication Data

Names: Hudd, Emily, author.
Title: The economic impact of COVID-19 / by Emily Hudd
Description: Minneapolis, Minnesota : Abdo Publishing, 2021 | Series: Core library guide to COVID-19 | Includes online resources and index.
Identifiers: ISBN 9781532194030 (lib. bdg.) | ISBN 9781644945001 (pbk.) | ISBN 9781098212940 (ebook)
Subjects: LCSH: Economics--Juvenile literature. | Finance, Personal--Juvenile literature. | Unemployment--Social aspects--Juvenile literature. | Business losses--Juvenile literature. | Quarantine--Juvenile literature. | Epidemics--Juvenile literature. | COVID-19 (Disease)--Juvenile literature.
Classification: DDC 330--dc23

CONTENTS

CLOSED FOR BUSINESS

Charity Salyers took a last look at her GT Mustang sports car. Then she sold it. She used the money to pay her employees during the COVID-19 pandemic. Salyers owned Vittles Restaurant in Smyrna, Georgia. She bought the restaurant in 2019, but it had been a popular place for 30 years. Many regular customers were elderly people. They counted on Vittles for a tasty meal.

However, the pandemic forced restaurants to close dining areas. Vittles was

Restaurant and small-business owners around the world faced the economic threat of COVID-19.

suddenly empty. Salyers had to cut back to just two workers. Vittles didn't usually offer takeout or delivery. But Salyers decided to offer both. She wanted to make sure her customers were getting fed. However, sales dropped sharply. By mid-April 2020, Salyers didn't have enough money to pay her employees. That is why she sold her Mustang. She got enough money to help the business survive another couple months. After that, the future of her restaurant was unknown.

Many businesses were affected by the pandemic. Small businesses

PERSPECTIVES

ONE PROBLEM LEADS TO ANOTHER

In a news broadcast in late March 2020, US president Donald Trump said, "Our country wasn't built to be shut down. . . . We cannot let the cure be worse than the problem itself." The cure he was talking about was closing businesses to slow the spread of the virus. Trump knew that this would hurt the economy. He didn't want the pandemic to lead to an economic crisis. However, experts said reopening businesses too soon could cause cases of COVID-19 to rise.

especially struggled. Some could only stay open by making big changes. Others weren't so lucky. By April, one in four small businesses in the United States had shut down temporarily. One in ten were at risk of closing forever. Unfortunately, people did not know when the crisis would end.

SLOWING THE PANDEMIC

COVID-19 is a disease caused by the coronavirus SARS-CoV-2. People infected with a coronavirus have respiratory problems. They might have trouble breathing. COVID-19 is mild for most people. But it can be deadly for others. The virus was first discovered in Wuhan, China, in December 2019. It spread to the United States by January 2020.

The virus spreads from person to person. When people cough, sneeze, or talk, the virus spreads through tiny droplets. It can enter the eyes, noses, or mouths of nearby people. These people become infected.

Coughing and sneezing can cause droplets of SARS-CoV-2 to spread to nearby people. Wearing a mask can help protect oneself and others.

Health officials recommended that people limit contact with others in order to slow the spread of the virus. This is known as social distancing or physical distancing. People who are social distancing stay at least 6 feet (1.8 m) apart. They avoid group gatherings.

Some countries also made shelter-in-place orders. This meant that people were asked to stay at home as much as possible. Authorities asked them to leave only for essentials such as groceries.

Social distancing and shelter-in-place orders helped people stay healthy. But there were drawbacks. Businesses and schools closed. The economy shut down.

ECONOMIES FALL ILL

Small and large companies were affected differently by COVID-19. Small businesses were more

ESSENTIAL BUSINESSES

Grocery stores, medical clinics, and home and auto repair services were considered essential businesses. Sports venues, gyms, movie theaters, and malls were nonessential. Determining which businesses were essential was difficult. State and local governments decided what would remain open. Businesses that were considered essential varied among regions. They included services that people relied on every day.

Many restaurants turned to curbside delivery and take-out options in order to stay in business.

likely to close. They depend on regular customers. Large companies can usually handle slow periods. Savings could help them stay afloat.

Financial experts predicted the pandemic would cause more bankruptcies than the Great Recession (2007–2009). Unemployment data showed the effect of COVID-19. The number of jobs dropped by 701,000 in March 2020. It was the first decline in the job market since September 2010. Approximately two-thirds of the lost jobs were in the hospitality industry. This includes jobs in bars and restaurants. Tens of thousands of retail jobs were also lost. These losses were only the beginning. By May 2020, 20.6 million jobs had been lost. This was more than twice the number of jobs lost during the Great Recession.

COVID-19 harmed local and national economies. Businesses didn't know if they would survive. But one fact was clear. The economy would look much different than before the pandemic.

FURTHER EVIDENCE

Chapter One talks about how COVID-19 changed people's lives and affected businesses. Identify the main point and some key supporting evidence. Then look at this website. Find a quote that supports the chapter's main point. Does the quote support a piece of evidence already in the chapter? Or does it add a new piece of information?

TIME FOR KIDS: IN IT TOGETHER

abdocorelibrary.com/covid-economic-impact

THE ECONOMY GRINDS TO A HALT

O n March 19, 2020, California became the first state to issue a stay-at-home order. California residents were told to leave their homes only for essentials. Some regions in California issued shelter-in-place orders. These orders also told people to stay at home. But shelter-in-place orders are usually made after natural disasters. Government officials wanted people to realize how dangerous the virus could be. By the end of March, 42 states had made stay-at-home or shelter-in-place orders.

California governor Gavin Newsom was the first to issue a statewide stay-at-home order during the COVID-19 pandemic.

State and local governments enforced these orders. Shelter-in-place orders were made to slow the spread of COVID-19. That way hospitals wouldn't become overwhelmed with cases of the virus.

CHANGES TO WORK LIFE

Shelter-in-place orders affected individuals and businesses. Only essential workers were allowed to travel for work. Some businesses made changes to fit social distancing guidelines.

Essential workers kept the community

Parents working from home often had to care for and teach their children in addition to doing their jobs.

running. They included health-care workers, grocery workers, and delivery drivers. But their work was risky. They interacted with many people. They could become sick. Then they might spread the virus to others.

Many people with office jobs could keep working. They use computers. They can do remote work. This means they can work from home. But remote work can be difficult. Adults had to find a space to work. They needed a good internet connection.

Many people who couldn't work from home lost their jobs. Employers could no longer pay them. Restaurant servers depended on tips. Entertainers depended on crowds. Construction jobs had to be done on-site.

PERSPECTIVES

DISNEY DROPS NUMBER OF WORKERS

Approximately 43,000 workers from Disney World in Florida were furloughed in April after Disney theme parks closed. Being furloughed is being out of work for a period of time. Many employees are able to use health benefits during this time. And they can come back to the job later. Furloughing is different from getting laid off because getting laid off is permanent. However, employees rarely go back to the same job after being furloughed.

INDUSTRIES HIT THE HARDEST

Governments told people not to travel. The tourism industry suffered. The United Nations World Tourism Organization (UNWTO) predicted a decrease of 300 to 450 billion dollars from the

An outbreak of COVID-19 on the cruise ship *Zaandam* caused many passengers to fall ill.

previous year. That would be a drop of approximately 30 percent.

Airlines and airports suffered. LAX, the main airport in Los Angeles, California, was the fourth busiest airport in the world before the pandemic. On April 17, 95 percent of its flights were canceled.

Industries that relied on travel also struggled. Azim and Navroz Saju owned and managed 18 hotels in Florida. They depended on government loans during the pandemic. Azim feared what would happen to their business if travel restrictions continued for several more months.

UNEMPLOYMENT AND MARKET CRASH

The United States reached an all-time high for unemployment. The pandemic erased nearly all job gains since the Great Recession. Approximately 22.4 million jobs had been added since that year. But in the four-week period leading up to April 11, 2020, more than 22 million people filed for first-time unemployment. This marked the worst four-week period in US history. The old record was set in 1982. That year, 2.7 million people filed for unemployment in a four-week period.

The effects of the pandemic were also seen in the stock market. Many companies allow people to buy small parts of the company. These parts are called stocks. The price of a stock goes up if the company does well. It drops if the company does poorly. The stock market tracks stock prices. Stock prices dropped sharply during the pandemic. The stock market crash

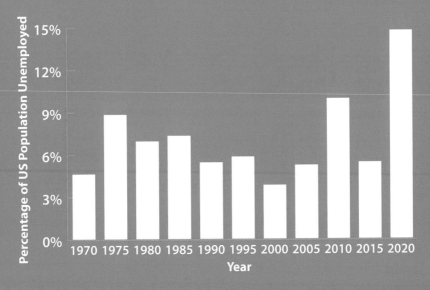

UNEMPLOYMENT LEVELS

For more than 50 years before the pandemic, less than 11 percent of the US population was unemployed. In April 2020, the number spiked. How does this graph illustrate the text? Does it help you understand the economic crisis?

began March 9, 2020. On March 23 the stock market hit a 52-week low.

The pandemic affected individuals and huge corporations. Tourism and travel industries were hit hard. Unemployment numbers and stock market prices showed the economic crisis. Many people lost their jobs. Others continued to work despite risks.

THE GOVERNMENT TAKES ACTION

The US government responded to the pandemic on March 6, 2020. It passed an $8.3 billion aid package. The money mainly went to state and federal health departments. They used the money to help prepare for an outbreak. They purchased medical supplies and gave loans to businesses.

But the country needed more aid. On March 18, lawmakers signed another bill. It provided free COVID-19 testing to people. It also gave food assistance and unemployment

Treasury secretary Steven Mnuchin was one of many federal officials who helped create financial aid plans for COVID-19 relief.

benefits to more people. It offered paid sick leave for certain workers. Paid sick leave allowed workers to stay home and quarantine. They did not have to go to work and risk infecting others. Still, more help was needed.

BILLS HELP PEOPLE AND ECONOMY

President Donald Trump signed the CARES Act on March 27. The name stood for Coronavirus Aid, Relief, and Economic Security Act. This package provided $2.3 trillion to help the economy. It included several types of aid to help people and businesses.

The CARES Act included small-business loans, tax cuts, and more unemployment benefits. It gave

BANKS TRY TO HELP

Banks worked with the government to help people. People with loans need to make regular payments to the bank. A loan is money given to someone. This money needs to be paid back over time. In some cases, banks allowed people to skip loan payments on money borrowed from the bank. Or they extended loans or changed parts of the deal to be more affordable.

WHERE CARES ACT MONEY WENT

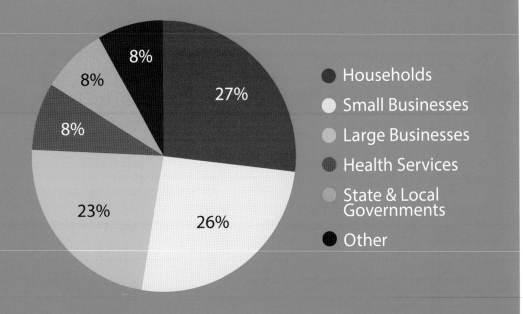

- Households
- Small Businesses
- Large Businesses
- Health Services
- State & Local Governments
- Other

8%
8%
8%
27%
23%
26%

The US government passed several bills to help those struggling financially from COVID-19. One of these bills was the CARES Act. Were you surprised by where the CARES Act money went? Did you expect certain groups to get more than others? Explain your answer.

$150 billion to state and local governments. It also gave direct payments to taxpayers. Most families received $1,200 per adult and $500 per child. People with high incomes received less aid. The payments encouraged people to spend money. Extra spending could help more businesses survive.

PERSPECTIVES

GETTING GOVERNMENT AID IS NOT EASY

In just three weeks, more than 30,000 people in Alaska lost their jobs. They called Alaska's Department of Labor. The department is in charge of job-related laws and programs. But the number of callers overwhelmed the system. The state tried to hire more workers for the unemployment office.

Symaron George filed for unemployment before the system got clogged. But she didn't get all the aid available to her. She was one of thousands of people waiting for full payment. She said, "My unemployment just barely covered my electric with $20 left over for two weeks. It's a scary and frustrating situation."

MORE FINANCIAL AID

The Paycheck Protection Program (PPP) was part of the CARES Act. Small businesses could apply for PPP loans to pay their staff and building fees. The PPP helped pay staff members even during a business shutdown. A business did not have to repay the loan if it used at least 75 percent of the loan to pay staff.

In one week, 70 percent of small-business owners

applied for PPP loans. The PPP ran out of funds on April 16. It had spent $349 billion on more than 1.6 million loans.

President Trump signed a fourth bill for coronavirus relief on April 24. This package was worth $484 billion. Most of the money was for additional small business loans. The PPP got another $300 billion. Approximately $75 billion went to hospitals. Another $25 billion was spent to increase testing for the disease. The government worked to keep the economy afloat.

EXPLORE ONLINE

Chapter Three discusses how the government helped people during the COVID-19 pandemic. Explore this website about government benefits. Compare and contrast this information with information from this chapter. What new information did you learn from the website?

CORONAVIRUS STIMULUS CHECKS ARE ON THEIR WAY: HERE'S HOW IT WORKS

abdocorelibrary.com/covid-economic-impact

GLOBAL IMPACTS

Shelter-in-place orders affected businesses and individuals. Production slowed. Shipments of goods were delayed. Companies in infected areas made less money than usual. For example, Apple had suppliers in 25 countries. Problems would occur if one link of their supply chain shut down or slowed. Apple's main factory for making iPhones was in China. The factory closed due to the pandemic. Apple's ability to get iPhones to customers suffered.

The outbreak of COVID-19 damaged the ability of large businesses such as Apple to make products. **27**

COVID-19 also affected people's ability to spend money. Stores closed. People were told to stay indoors. They had to use online shopping and delivery instead. The pandemic caused major lifestyle changes. Many avoided big purchases such as a home or car.

The oil industry also struggled. People canceled travel plans. They were told to stay home as much as possible. The need for gasoline dropped. Oil prices fell.

OIL PRICES DROP

Some oil nations in the Middle East and Africa decreased oil production. They matched production to the lower need for oil. They agreed to reduce their daily output by 9.7 million barrels. That is nearly 10 percent less than what they usually produced each day. But Russia and Saudi Arabia increased their production. They made more oil than people needed. Oil prices dropped as a result. On April 20, 2020, the supply of oil was greater than the demand. As a result, oil prices were negative for the first time in US history.

Popular tourist destinations such as the Colosseum in Italy had fewer visitors as people limited travel.

NATIONAL ECONOMIES

China's economy had been growing since 1976. It was worth $14 trillion in 2019. After the pandemic started, China's economy stopped growing for the first time in nearly 50 years. Chinese factories closed, and production slowed. Other nations pulled back from importing Chinese goods.

Italy's economy also suffered. Italy is one of the most popular tourist destinations in Europe. Tourism makes up approximately 13 percent of the country's economy. Due to COVID-19, Italy expected to have 28.5 million fewer tourists in 2020 than the previous year.

INTERNATIONAL TRADE

International trade was hurt as nations dealt with the virus. Countries wanted to make sure they had enough supplies. Australia stopped exporting supplies such as hand sanitizer. Switzerland relaxed rules about importing medicine, medical supplies, and protective gear. It needed more of these supplies to fight the disease.

Some countries began producing medical supplies themselves. Car and vacuum manufacturers started making ventilators. Clothing factories in the United States began making masks. This way the United States did not need to rely on other countries for these supplies.

Some car manufacturing factories were converted to produce ventilators.

Economies around the world faced challenges. The pandemic affected how people spent money. It had a greater effect on international trade than the Great Recession had. The impacts were likely to last long after the pandemic ended.

STRAIGHT TO THE
SOURCE

The pandemic caused Pope Francis, leader of the Catholic Church, to suggest a universal basic wage. It is a regular payment from the government to all its citizens. He said:

> *Many of you live from day to day, without any type of legal guarantee to protect you. . . . Small farmers, construction workers, dressmakers, the different kinds of caregivers: you who . . . have no steady income to get you through this hard time . . . and the lockdowns are becoming unbearable.*

> *This may be the time to consider a universal basic wage which would acknowledge and dignify the noble, essential tasks you carry out. It would ensure and concretely achieve the ideal, at once so human and so Christian, of no worker without rights.*

Source: "Pope Proposes Considering a 'Universal Basic Wage.'" *Catholic News Agency*, 12 Apr. 2020, catholicnewsagency.com. Accessed 15 May 2020.

WHAT'S THE BIG IDEA?

Take a close look at this passage. What is Pope Francis's hope for society following the pandemic? How does he think those with low pay should be treated? Does he focus on additional aspects of workers other than their pay?

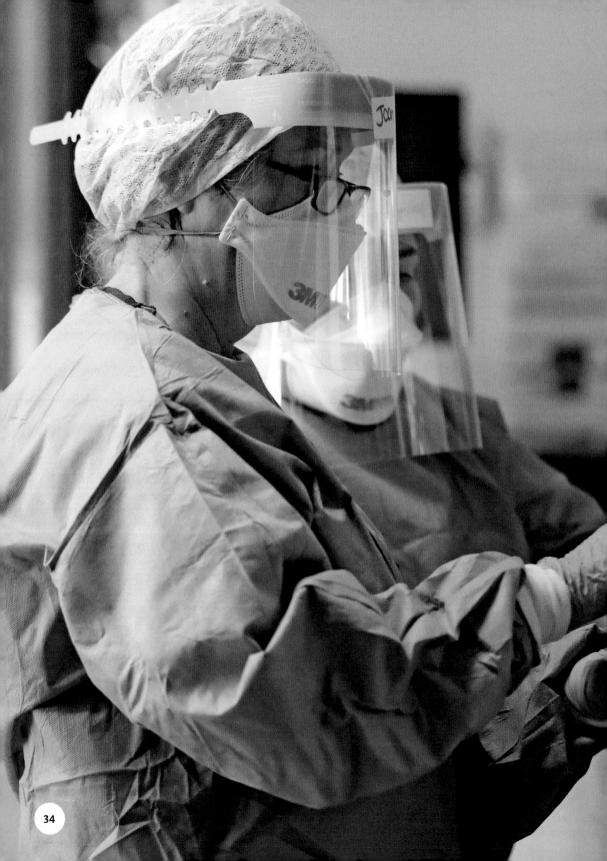

A NEW NORMAL

ndustries had to adjust to COVID-19. Many companies cut back on employees. But some hired more people. Delivery needs skyrocketed. Companies such as Amazon and Instacart needed more workers. Grocery stores and pharmacies also hired new employees.

Hospitals were short-staffed in some areas and overstaffed in others. They needed many employees to treat COVID-19 patients. Retired health-care professionals came back to work in some hospitals. But nonessential surgeries

Many hospitals were short-staffed. They needed more workers to treat the large number of COVID-19 patients.

Many people relied on telehealth services for treatment to avoid contact that could spread disease.

and procedures were delayed. Specialists in those areas faced job loss.

LASTING CHANGES FOR THE WORKPLACE

Experts believed remote work would continue after offices reopened. Some companies were as successful working from home as they were in the office. Companies were likely to continue offering flexible hours and work-from-home options after the pandemic.

The medical field also saw an increase in telehealth services. Telehealth provides patients with virtual medical care. It had been used in rural areas for several years, but it boomed during the pandemic. People were able talk to a doctor while at home. Patients could describe symptoms, receive a diagnosis, and even get a prescription. Many believed telehealth services would remain after the pandemic ended.

PERSPECTIVES

NOT GAME OVER

Dr. Anthony Fauci was the director of the US National Institute of Allergy and Infectious Diseases during the pandemic. He emphasized that people needed to be careful during reopening. Reopening did not mean the pandemic was over. He said, "You can call it the new normal, you can call it whatever you want, but even if you are in phase one, two, three, it's not 'OK, game over.' It's not."

BRIGHT FUTURE FOR TRAVEL INDUSTRY

After months of limited travel, experts believed people would be eager to explore. People might travel to places around the world. Local travel was also expected to increase. Supporting destinations close to home helps local businesses. Researchers hoped people would be more aware of where they spent their money.

DEBATING WHEN TO REOPEN

People debated when to reopen businesses. Reopening could cause more outbreaks. But keeping businesses closed would further harm the economy. By mid-April, protesters in several states wanted to reopen local economies. They pressured governors and President Trump to ease restrictions. Protesters wanted the freedom to return to their jobs.

FUTURE OUTLOOK

By May 20, 2020, all states that had made shelter-in-place orders began easing restrictions. The number of new cases had decreased throughout the

Some states began to slowly reopen restaurants and businesses beginning in May 2020.

United States. More COVID-19 tests were available. These factors encouraged governors to begin reopening businesses.

The federal government recommended reopening in three phases. Social distancing was to be followed during every stage. However, these practices would become less strict in the later phases.

In the guidelines proposed by the federal government, gyms and movie theaters were among the first places that could reopen. These places have more open space that lets visitors practice social distancing. Many states created individual reopening plans. Dine-in restaurants and retail stores reopened but limited the number of customers. Employees also needed to regularly clean their businesses and provide sanitization products to visitors. The federal government suggested schools and youth activities resume during the second phase. States hoped to allow visits to nursing homes during the third phase. People in nursing homes are more vulnerable to severe cases of COVID-19. But a sudden spike in new cases in late June caused many states to pause reopening plans.

Despite setbacks, many believed the economy would heal. Global stock prices rose in June. People on social media encouraged others to support small businesses. Financial experts predicted that the worst economic effects of COVID-19 were over. The economy would recover with time.

STRAIGHT TO THE
SOURCE

US financial expert Seema Shah spoke about unemployment in an interview in April 2020. She warned that economic struggles were not over at that point:

> *While today's jobless numbers are down on last week, they still mean that all the job gains since the financial crisis have been erased. What's more, with many workers . . . not included in these numbers, labor market pains may be even worse than these numbers suggest.*

> *Concerns for the second half of the year may be underestimated. Although governments are looking to lift lockdowns, the re-opening of economies will be only gradual, compounding financial strains . . . and suggesting a slower economic recovery.*

Source: "The US Economy Has Erased Nearly All the Job Gains Since the Great Recession." *CNBC*, 16 Apr. 2020, cnbc.com. Accessed 15 May 2020.

CONSIDER YOUR AUDIENCE

Review this passage closely. Consider how you would adapt it for a different audience, such as your younger friends. Write a blog post conveying this same information for the new audience. How does your new approach differ from the original text, and why?

FAST FACTS

- COVID-19 is a disease caused by a virus called SARS-CoV-2. SARS-CoV-2 is a type of coronavirus. Coronaviruses cause respiratory problems.

- SARS-CoV-2 spreads easily from close human contact. The virus can fly through the air in tiny droplets. Therefore, the best way to slow the spread of the virus is by social distancing. Social distancing reduces close contact with others.

- Many businesses were affected by the COVID-19 pandemic, but small businesses especially struggled.

- Many businesses temporarily closed to meet shelter-in-place guidelines. Protesters wanted nonessential businesses to reopen. Some wanted to return to their jobs. But reopening businesses too soon could cause more outbreaks.

- Restrictions changed individual behavior and affected local, national, and global economies. Tourism, airlines, and hotels were some of the industries that were hit the hardest.

- Due to COVID-19, unemployment in the United States rose sharply. In a four-week period ending April 11, 2020, more than 22 million people filed for unemployment.

- From March 6 to April 24, the US government passed four coronavirus relief packages. They included nearly $3 trillion in aid for unemployment, small businesses, hospitals, payments to individuals, and more.

- Many employees began working from home during the pandemic. Remote work may be a lasting change even after offices are allowed to reopen.

- Telehealth, or telemedicine, is when patients get medical care via phone, video, or app. Many people received this form of care during the COVID-19 crisis.

STOP AND
THINK

Surprise Me

Chapter Two discusses how businesses changed during the pandemic. After reading this book, what two or three facts about workers and businesses during this time did you find most surprising? Write a few sentences about each fact. Why did you find each fact surprising?

Say What?

Studying diseases and the economy can mean learning a lot of new vocabulary. Find five words in this book you've never heard before. Use a dictionary to find out what they mean. Then write the meanings in your own words, and use each word in a new sentence.

Take a Stand

People disagreed about how soon businesses should reopen during the pandemic. What do you think? Should businesses have been able to open if they followed social distancing guidelines? Or should businesses have stayed closed until widespread testing confirmed a decrease in cases? Why?

Why Do I Care?

Maybe your family does not own a business. But that doesn't mean you can't think about businesses and the economy. How has the disease affected countries around the world? How might your life be different if certain businesses never reopened?

GLOSSARY

bill
a document that may be
signed into law

export
to sell or send products to
another country

hospitality
having to do with an activity
or business related to serving
guests, such as in hotels
and restaurants

import
to buy or bring in products
from another country

loan
money borrowed from a
bank that has to be paid
back over time

pandemic
a disease that spreads across
the world

prescription
medication given by a doctor

remote work
work that can be done at
home or off-site

respiratory
having to do with the lungs
or breathing

supply chain
a group of businesses
involved in making different
parts for one product

ventilator
medical equipment that
helps people breathe

ONLINE RESOURCES

To learn more about the economic impact of COVID-19, visit our free resource websites below.

Visit **abdocorelibrary.com** or scan this QR code for free Common Core resources for teachers and students, including vetted activities, multimedia, and booklinks, for deeper subject comprehension.

Visit **abdobooklinks.com** or scan this QR code for free additional online weblinks for further learning. These links are routinely monitored and updated to provide the most current information available.

LEARN MORE

Hustad, Douglas. *World Leaders during COVID-19*. Abdo Publishing, 2021.

Marciniak, Kristin. *The Flu Pandemic of 1918*. Abdo Publishing, 2014.

INDEX

About the Author

Emily Hudd lives in Minnesota with her husband. She enjoys writing books for students. When she isn't writing, she is often reading or staying active.